BLISTRA
THE SEA DRAGON

SEA QUEST

BY ADAM BLADE

ORCHARD

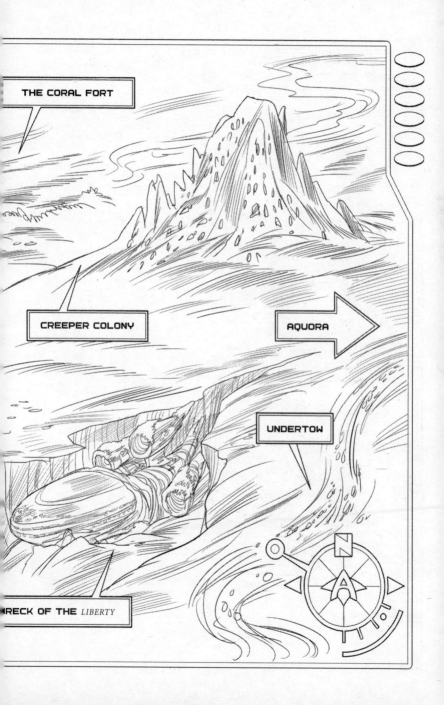

>TRANSMISSION FROM THE STARSHIP
LIBERTY

Any who threaten the SS *Liberty*
must die.

For 2,000 years I have lain at the
bottom of the ocean, forgotten.
For 2,000 years I have guarded my
ship. But my duty will never end:
analyse, react, destroy. Time may
have corroded my circuits, but I
have only grown more determined.

Now I have built four weapons to
aid me in my mission — creations
so powerful, nothing can stand
in their way. Enemies of the SS
Liberty beware. I will never stop
hunting you.

All threats must be terminated!

CHAPTER ONE

STARSHIP TRASH

"Spanner, Max?" asked Rivet. Max glanced up from the open panel in the dashboard of his sub, a bundle of trailing wires in his hand. His dogbot had a spanner clamped between his iron jaws.

"Thanks, Riv," said Max. "But I don't need it." Chewing his lip, he twisted some of the wires back together. "I'll just re-route the surplus power to boost the engines..."

Max eased the thruster control forward,

and the *Silver Porpoise* accelerated through the water, pushing him back against the cushioned seat. Yes!

He spoke into his mic. "The engines are ready to go, Lia."

"Good – let's not waste any more time," she said in the earpiece of Max's headset.

Through the plexiglass canopy, Max saw Lia lean forward on the back of Spike, her pet swordfish. Spike put on a burst of speed to overtake the sail sub, sending Lia's long, silver hair streaming out behind her in the water.

Normally she'd have made a quip about Max's reliance on technology, but this was no time for jokes.

Max looked forwards, past the nose of the sail sub, and his eyes narrowed. The starship *Liberty* was up ahead, speeding away from them. Its colossal disk-shaped body seemed to fill the ocean. The ancient spaceship, now repaired after lying wrecked on the ocean floor for two thousand years, was being piloted by its computer. But the artificially intelligent system, which called itself 'Iris', had become deranged after damage to her circuits. Now she was steering the *Liberty* towards Aquora, intent on destroying Max's home city.

With its power core broken, Aquora was defenceless. The vital water-filtration system was out of action too, and its people were already facing death by dehydration. Max swallowed down a feeling of nausea.

I must stop the Liberty *and restore Aquora's power. The drinking water supplies won't last for much longer.*

Max and Lia were racing against time to find four essential elements, originally part of the *Liberty's* engine, needed to restart the city's damaged power core. Iris had used the elements to super-power her deadly Robobeasts. So far, Max and Lia had defeated three beasts and retrieved three elements, Flaric, Magnetese and Blinc. They just needed the fourth element, Infernium.

Max glanced at the energy tracker that his mother, Niobe, had given him to locate the elements. The slim tablet had already led him to the wrecked *Liberty* and to Iris's Robobeasts. Now it was telling him that the Infernium was somewhere on the *Liberty* – probably, if their adventures so far had been anything to go by, stored within the body of another deadly Robobeast.

Max realised with relief that the *Silver Porpoise* was gaining on the *Liberty* at last. But his elation quickly drained away. He had acquired excellent underwater vision when Lia had given him the Merryn Touch, and he began to make out shapes scuttling on the starship's surface.

Creepers!

Max shuddered at the sight of the ant-like marine creatures. Creepers in the Delta Quadrant, where Max came from, were small and harmless. But here in the Primeval Sea, they had mutated. The smallest of these mutated creepers were as big as Rivet and they were all as aggressive as maddened wasps. Iris had enslaved the creeper queen by implanting a chip on the creature's neck. The queen was firmly under Iris's control, and through her, Iris could command every sea ant in the swarm!

Hundreds of the black-bodied worker creepers had patched up the breaches in the *Liberty's* hull with the glue-like resin secreted from their jaws. Guarding the workers were bigger, deep-red bodied soldier creepers, waving their long, vicious mandibles.

Suddenly Lia's voice broke through his earpiece. "Look out, Max! It's firing something!"

Max could see something shooting out from the tail of the *Liberty*.

"It's rubbish!" he shouted to Lia. "The *Liberty's* pumping the bilges. Get Spike out of the way. Quickly!"

Max veered to the left, trying to dodge the foul stream. But in moments they were engulfed by the black, oily water. Max leant forwards, squinting to see through the filthy clouds. Something green and slimy splattered on the cockpit bubble and slid downwards.

Gross. This stuff could clog Lia's gills.

Max tried to catch a glimpse of his friend, but suddenly a piece of metal crashed into the plexiglass, inches from his nose. He flinched, and the sail sub lurched to the side. Max wrenched the steering

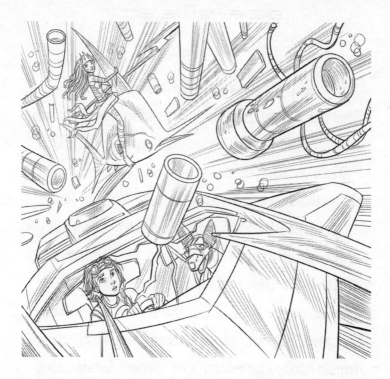

column to steady it. More lumps of debris
came flying towards them.

"Hold tight, Riv," said Max. "Magnetise
paws!"

"Yes, Max," replied Rivet, clamping his
front paws onto the floor of the sail sub. Max
fought to steer a safe path, but he couldn't
avoid all the pieces of junk, and the sail sub
spun dizzyingly under the onslaught.

It's like flying through a meteorite storm! But the meteorites are lumps of starship waste!

Rivet yelped as the sail sub lurched around. "Dirty, Max!"

"At least we're behind a watershield, Rivet. Lia's not so lucky. I wish I could see her!"

Max's knuckles were white by the time he coaxed the *Silver Porpoise* out of the tide of junk. Slowly he unclenched his hands from the steering wheel. But as the water cleared, he saw that they were not out of danger. The frantic flight had taken him off course, and now there was no sign of the *Liberty* or Lia. Instead, looming ahead was a towering wall of coral.

Desperately, Max twisted the controls to dodge the forest of branching coral columns. He fought to bank the *Silver Porpoise* up and away from the cliff. Shoals of multicoloured fish flashed across the sail sub's headlamps as they darted out of the way, and Max glimpsed clusters of glowing tentacles disappearing into dark rocky hollows.

For a moment he thought he was going to make it, but the turn was too tight. The small craft slammed into the wall of coral. Its belly scraped across the stony surface. Fragments of coral exploded around the cockpit, and over the terrible grating noise, Max heard the engines cut out.

The sail sub skidded off the edge of the coral stack, drifting in the open water. The indicators on the control panel were still, and the engines were silent. Holding his breath, Max pressed the starter motor. Nothing! Max slammed a hand against the controls.

"That's a bad sign," said Lia's voice in his ear, and Max looked up and smiled with relief to see his friend steering Spike in front of the viewing screen. There was a dark bruise already forming on her arm.

"Lia! Are you hurt?"

Lia shook her head. "Only one or two scratches. Spike got me through safely. What's the damage to the sail sub?"

"Critical damage to the engines!" said Max, grimacing. "It'll take ages to fix."

Max suddenly realised that the *Liberty* had stopped moving and was still in sight.

Is she damaged too?

"What's that?" said Lia, pointing.

The *Liberty* was aiming a shaft of purple light ahead of itself, and the energy beam was spiralling outwards, spreading through the water to create a vertical disk of spinning, glowing current. "It looks like a whirlpool," said Max. "But standing on its edge. And growing – fast!"

"Creepers, Max!" warned Rivet.

Dozens of the red soldier creepers were

detaching themselves from the *Liberty*. As they dropped off the hull, they opened fins along the length of their legs and began to swim. To Max's horror, the squadron of huge sea ants was headed towards him and Lia, their mandibles open and threatening.

They're coming to finish us off!

CHAPTER TWO

PORTAL

"Lia, get in the sail sub, quick!" There was a hiss as Max hit the airlock release. A second later, Lia clambered into the co-pilot seat, Rivet jumping down between them to make way.

"Spike, get out of here!" Lia shouted to the swordfish, who was still hovering in front of the viewing screen. With a swish of his tail he was gone, and not a moment too soon. *Thud.* The first soldier creeper landed on the cockpit bubble and stared through the watershield. Max shivered in the cold gaze of its bulbous eyes. The creeper opened its sharp pincers and aimed the blades at the edge of the watershield.

It's like an old-fashioned tin-opener…and we're the tin!

The little two-seater sail sub rocked as more creepers landed. They squealed as

they settled, and their feet skidded over the metal plating of the hull. Goosebumps prickled on Max's neck. Now he could see nothing through the watershield but dozens of triangular heads scraping their dreadful jaws over the plexiglass.

Screech! At the sound of tearing metal a jet of water fired through the cockpit, hitting Rivet and sending him flying. Lia grabbed him.

"Rivet scared!" the dogbot whined.

A second creeper bit through the hull, sending another high-pressure leak jetting across the cockpit. "We've got to get out of here!" Max shouted over the rush of water. Quickly, he stowed the energy tracker in the chest pouch on his deepsuit. Then he turned to Lia. "We'll have to use the hatch!"

"But how? The creepers are blocking it!"

Max tinkered with the bundle of wires

he'd used to reroute the extra power to the engines. "If I can send an electric pulse to the outer shell, it might stun them—"

"Giving us time to swim clear," interrupted Lia. "Can you do it?"

"No problem!" Quickly Max strapped on his hyperblade and grabbed the box containing the elements.

The sailsub shuddered again, and another gush of water surged into the cockpit, almost knocking the box out of Max's hands. Fumbling, he managed to stowed it in Rivet's back-compartment. "Guard it well, Riv! Are we ready?"

"Yes, Max!" Rivet barked.

"Ready!" said Lia, waiting by the hatch.

Max twisted two wires together. A bluish light engulfed the dome of the *Silver Porpoise*. The shimmering haze flowed over the creepers on the sub's surface, turning the creatures a sickly violet colour. They shuddered and dropped away.

"Now!" yelled Max, grabbing Rivet's collar.

The three of them erupted through the hatch. Max took a gulp of the warm seawater. Once again he was grateful for the gills that had appeared on his neck when Lia gave him the Merryn Touch.

Dazed creepers floated around the sailsub, motionless. Then, from the corner of his eye, Max saw a creeper twitch its legs. It launched itself at Lia. She yelled and struggled as its front pair of legs wrapped powerfully around her body. The sea ant's head pulled back, opening its mandibles wide, ready to bite through her neck.

Pow! There was a blur of movement, and Spike's sword slammed the creeper away from Lia. The Merryn princess jumped onto the swordfish's back.

"Others are waking up!" cried Max, batting a creeper aside and stabbing at another with his hyperblade. Rivet was protecting Max's back, snapping his powerful jaws at creepers coming from behind.

"Max!" shouted Lia. "The *Liberty*!"

Max glanced up in time to see the *Liberty* fire its thrusters, powering into the purple whirlpool. The starship hung motionless near the edge for a moment. It shivered and blurred as if they were seeing it through a heat-haze. Then it streamed towards the bright centre of the spinning vortex, and vanished. Max gasped.

A portal. But where does it lead?

To Max's horror, the outside edge of the whirlpool began to fold in towards the centre. "We need to get through that portal!" cried Max urgently.

Max grabbed Rivet's collar, and the

dogbot set off, dragging Max with him. Lia darted forward on Spike's back. Side by side, they shot towards the whirlpool, leaving the creepers behind.

They passed over the edge of the vortex, and Max heard a faint high-pitched hum. Every inch of his skin tingled, and the hairs on the back of his head lifted. He was engulfed in a rippling, purple landscape surrounding a bright centre of blue-white light. Max couldn't feel any movement, but that central eye was growing bigger and brighter by the moment.

What happens now?

The light swallowed them up. Max felt his body stretch and thin like a piece of elastic. He closed his eyes against the glare, but it shone through his eyelids. Then it vanished, and Max felt as if his body had snapped back into shape.

Max opened his eyes. He was still holding

Rivet's collar, and they were surrounded by the familiar blue-green light of ordinary seawater. Lia was beside him on Spike's back, gently patting the swordfish's flank. She turned to Max, and he grinned, almost laughing with relief.

What a ride!

Suddenly, Max remembered the creepers. He twisted round, raising his hyperblade, but the ocean around them was empty. Max felt a pang of regret. "We've left the creepers behind, but we've left the *Silver Porpoise* behind too."

"We had no choice," said Lia gently.

Max nodded. Lia was right. *But we haven't lost the* Liberty.

The starship hung in the water, just ahead of them. *What's Iris up to?* Max wondered.

"I know where we are," said Lia. "I can taste the water. We're home, near Sumara."

Suddenly, Max understood. "I've read

that in outer space there are things called wormholes. They're like rips in space. If you find one you can travel millions of light-years across the galaxy, in just seconds."

"So that's what that portal was..." Lia said. "A kind of undersea wormhole!"

Just then, the *Liberty* shuddered. There was a flash of light deep within a shiny new set of thrusters that Max could see had been added to the back of the vessel.

Lia pointed silently. In the distance a dark vertical shadow reached from the ocean bottom to the surface. Aquora!

Max felt a jolt of horror. "Iris is heading to Aquora. She's going to attack the city!"

"We need help," said Lia. She closed her eyes and raised her fingers to her temples. A passing marlin suddenly turned and zoomed towards her, the big fish hanging in the water for a moment, before it sped away.

"I've sent him to Sumara," explained Lia. "My people will send help as soon as he reaches them!"

"Great," Max said. "I'll warn Dad. Come on, we need to catch up with Iris!"

Max hung onto Rivet's collar as they sped through the water, Lia and Spike at their side. Max pressed the communicator on his watch. "We're in range for radio transmission," he said, hopefully. Immediately, Callum appeared on the little video screen, his image flickering against the streaming water. His face looked drawn and tired, but he smiled when he saw his son. "Max!" he cried. "It's good to see you. Tell me everything!"

Quickly, Max told Callum about the *Liberty* and Iris. "We've retrieved three of the four elements. Now we just need the Infernium. But Iris is crazy, Dad," he said. "She thinks Aquora's a threat. She wants to destroy it!"

Callum's face turned ashen. "We still have no power. The city is defenceless. You are our only hope, Max. Our fate is completely in your hands!"

Max glanced up through the swirling water. He was speeding towards the *Liberty*, pulled along by Rivet, but he felt a knot of hopelessness. The ship suddenly looked unreachable.

It's picking up speed. How can I stop Iris now?

CHAPTER THREE

CAUGHT IN AMBER

Max stared at his father's stricken face and shrugged off his own despair.

I can't let him down. I must find a way to save Aquora!

Suddenly, Max had an idea, remembering Aquora's magnificent naval destroyer, the *Sea Hammer*. "There is a way, Dad!" Max burst out. "The *Sea Hammer's* new long-range defence torpedo."

"We can't do that, Max." Callum sighed.

"The prototype hasn't even been tested yet!

"Besides, if we torpedo the *Liberty*, we risk destroying the Infernium as well."

Max took a deep breath. "Don't worry about the Infernium. I'll get on board and get the element out before you attack. Please don't argue..." he added, as Callum began to protest. "We have no choice. Just pull the trigger, Dad!"

Callum hesitated. Then he shook his head reluctantly. "You're right," he said. "It will take time for the crew of the *Sea Hammer* to charge up the weapon, and lock it onto the *Liberty*. Once fired, I'd say the torpedo will take around ten minutes to reach your location." Callum looked worried. "I'd estimate you have twenty minutes before the torpedo hits. Do your best and then get out of there, whether you've got the Infernium or not. Good luck, son. I'm proud of you."

"Thanks, Dad. Good luck, too. Goodbye." Max signed off. Moisture was blurring the corners of his vision. *I hope this isn't the last time I see Dad's face.* Max wiped his eyes, gathering his courage. He called to Lia. "I have to get on board the *Liberty* and find the Infernium."

But Lia was looking past him. "Creepers! Coming this way."

Hordes of creepers, both black and red, were streaming out of a hatch on the *Liberty's* hull. "Stop swimming, Riv!" shouted Max. "They're attacking." He quickly drew his hyperblade.

Workers and soldiers. Dozens of them.

Lia was ready on Spike's back, spear in her hand. She was on Max's left, and Rivet was on his right. Together, they faced the creepers.

The sea ants had extended the fins on their legs and were swimming quickly, descending through the water towards Max and his friends. They spread out as they advanced. Max and Lia turned back-to-back to face as many as possible. In seconds they were surrounded, the creatures' mandibles clicking together in a nerve-jangling screech. Max steadied his hyperblade, adrenaline surging through him.

The first of the sea ants attacked, snapping its pincers at Max's face. Max swung his hyperblade, bashing the flat edge against its triangular head. The creature fell away, stunned. More creepers surged forwards, and Max swung again, felling three with a flurry of blows. Behind him, he knew Lia was stabbing with her spear, her swordfish wielding his sword.

A creeper attacked from below and Max batted it aside, spinning and whacking his hyperblade against more of the sea ants on the return swing.

There was a movement to Max's side, but before he could react, Rivet leapt past him and chomped his heavy jaws down on a soldier creeper. He shook his iron head once and tossed the writhing body away.

"Thanks, Riv," panted Max.

The sea was thick with creepers. Every time one fell, ten more came to take its place. Max was beginning to tire, and he could

hear Lia gasping with the effort of keeping the attackers at bay.

We can't fight forever!

Suddenly, Max heard Lia cry out. He whirled round in time to see a sea ant slamming its head like a battering ram against Spike's vulnerable gill cover. Spike lurched, and Lia tumbled from his back, her spear sailing out of her outstretched hand. Spike drifted, unconscious, but the creepers ignored him and turned on Lia. The Merryn girl was surrounded by vicious snapping mandibles.

Max hurried towards his friend, slashing furiously at the sea ants, Rivet protecting his back. For a moment Max thought he could reach Lia…but then one of the creepers opened its jaws over her head. Max could see something like saliva foaming from its mouth.

I can't save her!

But, to Max's surprise, the creeper didn't bite Lia. Instead, it spat a greasy amber blob from its jaws, onto the back of her head. Max realised that this was a worker creeper. The blob must be the resin the creepers used to build their hive and repair the *Liberty*.

"Urgh!" Lia was struggling, horrified, as the disgusting mess slithered down her body.

She put up her hands to shield her gills, but the resin set around her fingers like glue. "I can't move," she shouted.

Just then, a soldier creeper swung its heavy head at Rivet's rear end. Caught off balance, the dogbot tumbled head-over-heels, out of Max's field of vision.

Splat! Max felt a chill run from his shoulder to the tips of his fingers. Two worker sea ants had dropped resin onto his arm. He tried to swipe at the insects with his hyperblade but his elbow and wrist were frozen at his side.

More resin dribbled over his body, sea ants swarming around him. He tried to kick free, but his legs were stuck together! His torso went rigid as his shoulders and hips were immobilised too. His gills were clear, but that was little comfort.

I'm just like a bug trapped in tree resin... and soon to be dead!

"Here, Max!" called Rivet. The dogbot tried frantically to reach Max, but the

creepers just smashed him aside.

"Get back, Riv!" shouted Max. "Stay clear!"

If any resin gets into his joints, he's finished!

Rivet obeyed. A soldier creeper batted him aside, and he didn't try to fight his way back.

Max struggled to look at Lia. Like him, she was immobile, encased in the foul resin. Four worker creepers held her in their jaws, and Max cried out, expecting them to tear her apart. But instead, they began to carry her towards the *Liberty*. Max felt pincers wrap around his own limbs. His captors started to swim, holding him in their pitiless grip.

When they reached the *Liberty* a hatch near the tail opened to let them in. Lia was bundled inside, and the creepers carrying Max headed after her.

Max seethed with frustration.

I wanted to get onto the *Liberty*, and here I am! But I'm completely helpless!

CHAPTER FOUR
ON BOARD THE LIBERTY

The creepers were holding Max flat on his back, so he could only see the ceiling of the airlock. He heard the hatch close behind him, and the water in the airlock drained away with a slurping gurgle. A swell of hot, damp air surged over him, and Max could hear the sea ants' feet splashing through puddles as they set off through a maze of corridors.

Max tried to move his arms and legs but they were frozen in place, his hyperblade still clutched in his locked fingers. Luckily his mouth and nose were clear of resin, but his chest could barely move and his breath came in shallow gasps.

Max glanced across to where the creepers were carrying Lia. She was face down, and her silver hair hung in amber-plastered tangles over her face. Her body twitched as she struggled to free herself, but at least she could breathe too.

Thank Nemos for the Sepha!

Ever since Lia had eaten the Sepha's kelp, she had been able to breathe oxygen. Before that she'd needed to wear an amphibio mask to leave the water. Max knew that if Lia had been stranded on the *Liberty* without the kelp's bacteria in her gills, she would have quickly suffocated.

Max stared up at the ceilings of the endless corridors, as he was carried in by the insects.

The vessel was grey and rusted, and covered in barnacles and limp, lifeless sponges, stranded on board when the ship had been drained. Max could see smooth amber areas of resin patching up cracks in the knobbly surfaces.

Sealed with creeper resin to keep the ocean out. And to keep the air in. *But why is it so hot?* Sweat was pooling under Max's deepsuit and dripping off his neck. Condensation gathered everywhere. It ran down the walls and dripped from the ceiling, landing on Max's face.

Ugh! I can't even wipe it away!

At last the creepers stopped marching and let go of Max. He grunted as his stiff back hit the floor.

"*Oof!*" grunted Lia nearby, as the creepers dropped her face down. "Max! Are you there? I can only see the floor!"

"I'm here," muttered Max.

"Where are we?" asked Lia.

Max could turn his head a fraction, and strained to look around him. They were in a large chamber, which Max recognised immediately. They'd been here before, when the *Liberty* was still a wreck at the bottom of the sea, and they'd first met Iris. "We're in the engine room," he said. The walls were lined with rows of empty pods, which had

carried human settlers on their voyage from outer space to Nemos, two thousand years before. The room was full of equipment with huge cylinders and pipes running across the ceiling, all connected by complex ducts and cables. In the centre of the room was the huge spaceship engine, connected to the ceiling by a shaft. It was the twin of Aquora's energy core. All the equipment was dead and encrusted with marooned sea life.

The engine's still inactive. So how is the Liberty fuelling its thrusters?

Suddenly, a tiny metal capsule appeared from over Max's shoulder and hovered a few inches above his face. Max's eyes narrowed. "Iris!" he hissed.

"Are you pleased to see me?" replied a girl's voice. The silver capsule darted away and began to glow with a reddish sheen. Sparks and tiny lightning-bolts crackled from its surface and swirled outwards into a pulsating plasma shape. It solidified into the flickering image of a girl with a smooth fringe of dark hair. She looked about twelve years old, the same age as Max.

The liquid metal hologram was projected and held in place by the magnetic capsule, which now formed a shiny belt buckle on Iris's jumpsuit. "Hello, Max," she said, standing over him.

Lia grunted from her face-down position. "Ugh. I hear the plasmagram's back! Forgive me if I don't stand up and hug it!"

Iris smiled, but her green eyes flashed and turned red. "Your primitive slave is tiresome," she said to Max. "And you are a mess." Her freckled nose wrinkled. "Too much exercise... I detect human sweat."

"It's hot in here!" Max snapped back.

"You are correct," said Iris. "I'm sorry I can't offer you air-con. I had to drain the *Liberty* to operate her, but I keep the atmosphere just hot and wet enough for my creeper queen and her daughters to survive out of the water."

So the creeper queen's on board! Max felt his skin crawl at the thought of the enslaved and maddened creature.

"I am disappointed that my creepers have not yet brought me your robot pet," went on

Iris. "But I will soon find it. It will be useful for scrap metal."

Rivet! Iris hasn't captured him!

Iris went on, "Of course, you'll never get the Infernium. It is quite safe. I have everything I need to destroy your city. Aquora is a threat to the *Liberty*. It must be crushed!"

Max shivered. He knew Iris was crazy and paranoid, her circuits damaged, but he had to try and reason with her one more time. "Aquora isn't hostile," he said carefully. "My people have done nothing to hurt you. Please! You don't have to do this!"

Iris stood still, and her eyes flashed with a blue light.

She looks as if she's downloading information. She's thinking! Max felt a tiny bubble of hope in his chest.

"You're trying to trick me!" Iris said angrily. "My scanners have picked up a torpedo, locked onto the *Liberty*. Call it off. Now!"

Max thought quickly. *She's detected the* Sea Hammer's *defence torpedo… This could be my chance!* He looked steadily at Iris. "I can call it off," he lied. "The torpedo was fired from my father's ship. It's heading this way. But I have the technology to disengage it.

And I'll do it – if you give me the Infernium."

Iris studied him carefully.

Will she take the bait?

"Your feeble heart is beating too rapidly," said Iris coldly. "And your blink pattern also indicates that you are lying to me. You are in no position to make bargains."

"Fine!" Max said aloud. "Then we're all going to die. You and the *Liberty* are doomed!"

Iris shrugged. "Not all of us will die," said Iris. "I will survive through my capsule, which can hold my entire coding, even if the ship's mainframe is destroyed. My ship will live on – through me! And I will still have the means to destroy Aquora. My only regret is that you'll never see my ingenious Blistra in action..."

Lia interrupted her, "Blistra? What's that?"

"Be grateful you'll never know," said Iris.

"This way you will die in blissful ignorance. Goodbye." The liquid metal plasmagram was sucked back into the capsule. It whizzed out of the engine room. As she left, Iris's voice boomed out of the loudspeakers: "One hundred and twenty seconds to torpedo impact."

A countdown!

"One hundred and nineteen seconds...one hundred and-eighteen..."

Max shuddered with horror. *Iris has outmanoeuvred me! She's going to escape, and we're going to die...*

CHAPTER FIVE

COUNTDOWN TO IMPACT

The creepers followed Iris out of the room, leaving Max and Lia alone and helpless on the wet floor. Max started struggling with the binding resin again, but he couldn't move an inch.

It's hopeless!

The countdown continued. Max's muscles strained against the resin and his body ran with sweat. Suddenly, his left elbow shifted a little. Max increased his efforts. There was another tiny movement.

"Lia!" he hissed. "I think the heat is softening the resin."

"I feel it too," said Lia, grunting as she tried to move her hands. "But I still can't get free. Can you use your hyperblade?"

"No." Max sighed. "The resin on my fingers is too thick. The other hand is melting more quickly, but I need to speed it up. If I could reach my blaster…"

Max concentrated on moving his left arm.

It's like pushing against a brick wall.

Painfully slowly he brought his left hand towards the blaster at his waist. *There!* He groped for the trigger.

"It's glued in. I'm going to have to fire it through the holster!"

"Be careful," muttered Lia. "But hurry."

With a huge effort, Max tilted the blaster in its holster. He hoped the barrel was pointing in the gap between his arm and his body.

If not, I might shoot off my own leg…

He fired. A blast of heat seared down the length of his body. Max flinched, waiting for the pain, but it didn't come. Instead he felt a wave of relief as the resin loosened its grip on his right side. He flexed his leg and the resin bent and cracked at the knee. Carefully he tested his grip on the hyperblade. It worked! He slashed the hyperblade through the resin binding his feet together, rotating his ankles as movement returned.

"I'm free, Lia." He used the blaster to soften the resin down his left side and struggled to his feet. "I can melt the resin with the blaster and slash it apart with the hyperblade."

"Great! So maybe get this stuff off me. There's only a countdown going on."

"Ninety seconds…eighty-eight…"

Max quickly fired his blaster at the resin

encrusting Lia. Globules of it slid towards the floor. He sent an extra blast over her hands, releasing them from her neck. She sat up and threw Max a smile. "Thanks."

Quickly they blasted and scraped the sticky resin off themselves. "Let's get out of here," said Max.

"Seventy seconds..."

Suddenly, there was a deep rumble, and the engine room shuddered. Max raced to one of the giant portholes around the room. He could see part of the tail of the *Liberty*. The six huge sets of cylinders and pipes that had been attached to it had torn away, leaving jagged broken metal behind.

"The thrusters have disappeared!" cried Max. "No – they're there!" he added, as they loomed out of the shadow of the tail. They were coiled together, the shiny new portions entwined with the older duller parts, cylinder stacked on cylinder. The cluster reminded Max of a gigantic conical snail shell. It tumbled over itself as it span away from the ship.

"What's it doing?" asked Lia.

"It's transformed into some kind of vessel. I bet the Infernium's in those thrusters, and

Iris wants it safely away from here. I hope she succeeds. If the Infernium survives, there's still a chance for Aquora."

Lia nodded. "Some other Aquoran might be able to find it and save the city, if we fail."

"Sixty seconds..." said Iris's voice.

Max thumped the edge of the porthole. "There must be a way out of here!"

He scanned the room. The cryogenic pods that had carried the first settlers to Nemos were standing empty and useless. But – there! There was a long bulbous compartment at the base of one of the walls, with a grimy plexiglass window at the top. Through it, Max thought he could see the outline of a row of escape-pod-like vehicles.

"Follow me," he yelled to Lia. "Shield your eyes!" Max fired his blaster as he ran, and the plexiglass shattered into fragments. The escape pods under it still looked shiny and

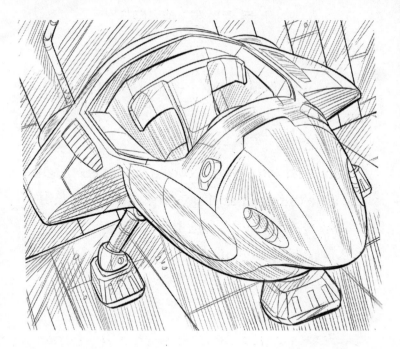

new. They were compact one-man vessels.

Suddenly, there was an ear-splitting screech. Max saw Lia go flying and slam against the side of one of the vehicles. Then something smashed into the back of Max's knees. His legs collapsed under him, and his hyperblade flew out of his hand. A weight landed on his back, knocking him to the ground and pinning him down. The furious screeching continued, inches from his ear,

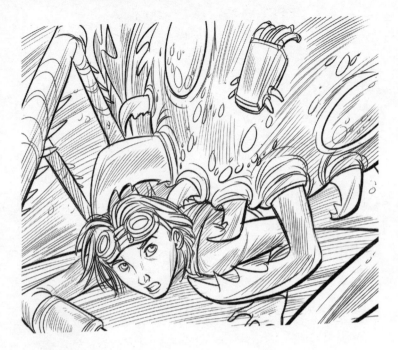

and then broke off into a series of horrible
grating clicks.

"It's the creeper queen," shouted Lia.

Max tried to twist over, but the queen's
claws dug into his back. At any moment, Max
expected the sharp pain of her mandibles
biting in his flesh.

Thwack! The queen's grip loosened and
Max rolled over to see her skidding across
the floor. "This makes a great club!" said Lia,

waving a hunk of barnacle-covered metal, broken away from a ventilation shaft.

"Thanks! But here she comes again," warned Max. The queen had turned back towards them. Her brown body was twice the size of one of the soldier ants, and the red chip on her neck bleeped steadily. Her knife-like claws and giant mandibles clattered as she advanced. Max's hyperblade was lying just a few inches away. He lunged for it, grabbing the hilt. At the same time the queen launched herself at Lia. Max twisted. He brought the hilt of the hyperblade down on the queen's head. *Crack!* Her legs crumpled, and she fell back, shaking her head. "Let's move!" yelled Max.

There was an exit door in front of the pod, the ocean visible beyond a small, round window. Max spotted a manual release button by its side.

"Ten seconds to impact!" Iris's automated voice sounded over the loudspeaker.

"Quick, into the pod!" Lia and Max leapt into the escape pod together, squeezing side by side onto the small open cockpit. Max leaned out of the craft, aimed his blaster at the control panel and pressed the trigger. The panel exploded, and the exit door slid open, filling the *Liberty* with water.

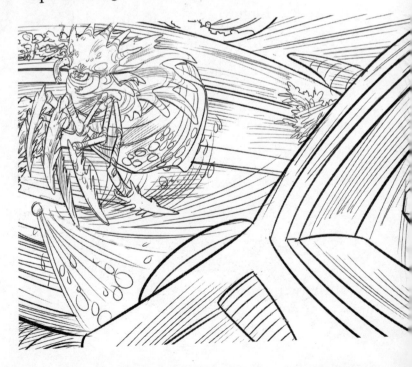

Max stared at the pod's controls, trying to figure them out.

"Five seconds to impact!"

He jabbed at a button, closing the cockpit cover. Then he hit the thrusters and the pod surged forward into churning ocean. "Propulsion systems engaged," said Max, grappling with the steering wheel. The little pod had been designed for space travel, and

Max had to fight to keep it steady in the water. He glanced back to catch a glimpse of the *Liberty*, and saw that the starship was already receding into the distance, the creeper queen just visible, swimming from the exit door.

We're clear!

Then Max saw the long-range defence torpedo speeding towards the *Liberty*. At this distance the weapon almost looked harmless, like a toy arrowhead shooting through the froth of water. Max craned his neck to watch as it exploded into the side of the starship. Max and Lia shielded their eyes. A bright blinding light flared across the sea. It was followed a beat later by a deafening roar and a surge of water. The pod went into a spin, and Max and Lia tumbled around inside the cramped space.

Frantically, Max tried to grab something

to steady himself, but there was nothing to hang onto. The escape pod was totally out of control!

There's nothing I can do!

Max's head slammed into the watershield, and everything went dark.

CHAPTER SIX

INFERNIUM

"Max! Wake up!" Max opened his eyes and saw Lia's blurry face up close. She was shaking him. He blinked, and she started to come into focus. "We need to get out, Max!"

Max took a deep breath. They were still in the escape pod, but it had stopped moving. He lifted a hand. "Okay, Lia. I'm awake."

"At last." Lia sighed.

Water was dripping into the escape pod through a crack in the watershield. *Thump!* Something skidded across the outside of the pod, and it rocked sickeningly. "What was that?" said Max, through a wave of nausea.

"A chunk of the *Liberty*! We need to move!" Lia grabbed Max's blaster and fired it at the watershield. The plexiglass shattered, and seawater rushed into the pod. It slapped Max back against his seat, but the flow of it across his gills woke him properly. He ducked out of the pod after Lia.

Outside, the water was dark with silt. Max could just make out the shadowy shape of the mangled ship in the distance. Lumps of debris from the explosion tumbled down and thudded into the seabed, churning up more sandy clouds.

"Look out!" cried Max. One massive fragment was plummeting down towards them! They dodged back, and the huge chunk landed inches away. But instead of settling harmlessly onto the seabed, it rolled back to rest against the pod, jamming Lia's leg against the hull.

Lia screamed with shock and began to struggle, pushing frantically at the lump of debris. Desperately, Max heaved against the metal, but it was too heavy.

It's no good! I can't move it!

"Found Max!" said a welcome voice.

Max whirled around. Rivet's headlights were beaming through the cloudy water as the dogbot dashed towards them.

"Rivet! Good dog!" cried Max.

Lia stopped struggling and scanned the ocean. "Spike should be here too. Where is he, Rivet?"

"Don't know, Lia. Sorry."

Lia slumped, looking defeated, and Max spoke quickly. "We'll find Spike later, Lia, I promise. But right now we need to get you free. Can you dig a hole so this lump of metal rolls away, Riv?"

"Yes, Max!" Quickly, Rivet swam down to the sea floor. Propellers churning, he set to work digging a trench with his paws. The sand tumbled back into the trench as he worked, but he kept at it. At last the lump of metal creaked and rolled and resettled a little way from the sub.

Max grabbed Lia and tugged her free. "Are you okay?"

Lia rubbed her leg and nodded. "Just bruised. Thanks, Max. And thank you, Rivet." She patted Rivet's head.

"You got here just in time, Riv," added Max.

Rivet wagged his metal tail. "Happy, Max!" he barked, and Max laughed.

Lia was scanning the water. "I hope Spike is okay."

"Don't worry, Lia," said Max gently. "I'm sure he will find us."

They swam away, dodging the last pieces of debris.

"What now, Max?" asked Rivet.

"Let's see," said Max. He slid the energy tracker out of the chest pouch of his deepsuit. With a grin, he showed the screen to Lia and Rivet. "It's picked up a trace! The Infernium hasn't been destroyed. That means there's still hope for Aquora." In fact…the signal was getting closer. Max scanned the ocean.

And then it appeared. Max recognised the massive coiled structure that he had seen leaving the starship, hurtling towards them. "It's the *Liberty's* thruster unit."

The huge entwined cylinders and pipes were changing shape again, beginning to unfurl. Giant clamps unhinged, folding outwards like massive petals. Panels slid over each other, and the metal fractured and became a covering of scales. Max watched with horror as the unit uncurled into a huge, legless body, swimming sinuously, like a snake. It had a tube-like snout, vicious spikes and burning yellow eyes at one end, and a whip-like tail at the other. Flat metal plates fanned out in a ruff around its neck, and massive wings stretched out from its sides.

It reminded Max of the dainty sea dragons he had seen swimming around Aquora. The harmless little fish were cousins of seahorses, and they disguised themselves as seaweed to escape predators.

But this giant doesn't need camouflage. It's a predator, not prey!

"A Robobeast!" said Lia.

Max nodded. "Iris's fourth. And I'll bet it's fuelled by Infernium!"

The Robobeast was very close now. The plasmagram of Iris was sitting on its neck, and her crazed red eyes were fixed on Max.

The mouth at the end of the Robobeast's tubular snout flared open. Deep in its throat, Max saw a spark ignite and grow.

Lia had seen it too. "It's a flame-thrower!"

Iris's voice boomed out as she rode the Robobeast towards them. "Very good, fish girl. A trace of Infernium creates flames a

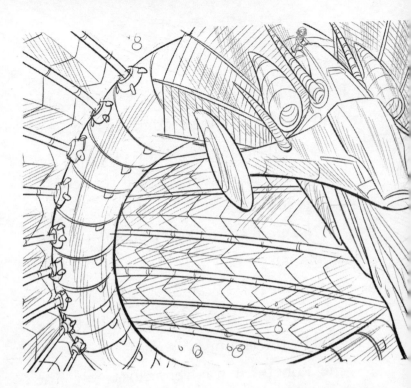

thousand times hotter than feeble Celerium fuel, able to burn underwater. Let me show you! Behold Blistra the Sea Dragon!"

As fire erupted from Blistra's mouth, Max grabbed Rivet's collar with one hand and Lia's arm with the other. "Go, Riv!" he yelled. Propellers whirring, the dogbot dragged them out of the way. The heat of the flames licked at Max's heels. *It won't miss us next time!*

"Quick, behind that debris," called Max. Rivet pulled Max and Lia behind a big piece of the shattered *Liberty*. Painfully hot water scalded Max's gills, and the metal debris radiated heat. After a while, Max peeked out. The Robobeast's mouth was closed. It glared at their hiding place.

Max turned back to Lia. "It must need time to recharge before it can fire again." But before they had a chance to flee, the colossal sea dragon appeared in front of them.

Iris glared at them. "You cannot survive against Blistra, and neither can your city."

"The *Liberty* has gone, Iris!" shouted Max. "There's no ship for you to protect, so you've nothing left to fight for. You can stop now!"

Iris's whole plasmagram body turned red and her eyes burned with maddened fury. "I AM the *Liberty*! And I will destroy Aquora."

"Aquora has never done you or the oceans any harm!" cried Max.

"You're mad!" shouted Lia.

Iris laughed. "I know exactly what I am doing!" she cried. "I'll take my leave of you now. Here come my creepers to finish off you and your slave!"

A wave of sea ants appeared around Iris. The crazed plasmagram pointed at Max and Lia and shouted, "Kill!" Then the Robobeast flattened its wings against its sides and turned, carrying Iris towards Aquora with a serpentine flick of its massive tail.

"Big ants, Max," said Rivet.

As one, the swarm of insects turned their triangular heads towards Max and Iris, and began to advance. Max grabbed his blaster and pressed the trigger. Nothing happened. "It's out of charge!" He pushed it back into its holster and grabbed his hyperblade.

"I need a weapon," said Lia. "I lost my spear when the creepers took us hostage." She picked something up from the sand.

Max raised an eyebrow at the thin, crooked piece of metal. "An antenna?"

"A makeshift spear," she said bravely.

Max steadied himself. "It will have to do," he said. "Those sea ants should watch out!"

They turned, back to back, to face the creepers. *This is a fight to the death!*

CHAPTER SEVEN

BATTLE FIRE

The creepers advanced on Max and Lia. They were already no more than a few feet away, their grating war cry setting Max's teeth on edge. He lifted his hyperblade, ready to slash as soon as they came close enough.

Then the ranks of creepers stopped swimming. Their leg fins folded down, and they stood still in the water. They began to shake their heads.

As if they're waking from a bad dream!

The confused creepers started to back

away. "They're not attacking!" said Max, puzzled. But Lia was staring past the creepers at something else. Max could just make out a wide band of shadow stretching through the water. It was coming towards them, fast. "What is it?" he hissed.

Lia laughed joyfully. "Your Breather eyes are still dim compared to mine, despite the Merryn Touch. It's Father!"

Merryn!

The full force of the Sumaran army was on its way. As they rode their swordfish closer, Max saw that the warriors were fully armed, and the edges of their coral spears glinted. He had never felt so pleased to see Lia's people.

Lia waved wildly. "You came!" she cried. Beaming proudly, she turned to Max. "They must be using their Aqua Powers to control the creepers. Look! They're backing off!"

"But what about the queen?" said Max.

"Iris controlled her and her swarm through the implanted chip."

The Merryn princess grinned. "I think my father has rescued her," she said, pointing. Max saw King Salinus riding into view. He wasn't riding his swordfish. Instead he was on the back of the creeper queen!

The queen looked like she had been wounded when the *Liberty* exploded. Her armoured hide was battered, and one of her mandibles had been blasted off. But she was calm, and she had stopped screaming. In fact, Max realised, all the sea ants had fallen silent.

King Salinus held up the chip that Iris had implanted into the creeper queen. "I managed to prise it out," he said. "Now the creeper queen is free of the evil that enslaved her, and she and her swarm are able to respond freely to our Aqua Powers." He reached over and hugged Lia. "The marlin brought us your message, Lia. And soon after that, someone else appeared... Here he is!"

"Spike!" cried Lia, throwing her arms around her swordfish.

Spike trilled happily and turned a somersault in the water. "I'm so glad you're here." Lia laughed, jumping onto his back and hugging him again. "I was worried about you."

Max was looking at the energy tracker. "King Salinus, we need to follow the Robobeast. Iris – the Artificial Intelligence system that controlled the creepers – she's totally insane and she's going to use Blistra to destroy Aquora! After that she'll turn on Sumara!"

King Salinus nodded. "Then we have no time to lose! Lead the way!"

Max grabbed Rivet's collar. He glanced behind as Rivet set off, pulling him through the water towards Aquora. King Salinus was following on the creeper queen. She let out a flurry of clicks, and the sea ants fell into ranks. Lia, on Spike's back, swam next to Rivet. Max shot her a broad grin.

It feels good to have an army!

But a few minutes later, the sight of the terrible Robobeast gliding through the water towards Aquora shook Max's confidence again. Blistra stopped its sinuous underwater flight. As Max watched, it spread its wings and lifted its body vertically in the water. Then the Beast turned, spinning gracefully on the tip of its tail, before dropping down with its terrible snout pointed towards Max and his companions. Iris glared at them from its back, her eyes glowing with furious red light.

Max turned to King Salinus. "Its mouth is a flame-thrower, and it breathes fire so hot it boils the sea!" he explained. "If you see its mouth open, flee!"

King Salinus nodded. He zoomed along the line of Merryn fighters, warning them of the danger. Then he turned to the Robobeast, which was writhing and snapping its jaws in front of the Sumaran army. King Salinus raised his spear. "Attack!" he bellowed.

The front line of warriors shot forward, thrusting their spears at the vulnerable joints between the Robobeast's metal plates. But the spearheads fell away harmlessly. Blistra roared, swiping its tail, smashing Merryn warriors through the water, and snapping at their swordfish mounts.

"Hold! Warriors, fall back!" The king laid

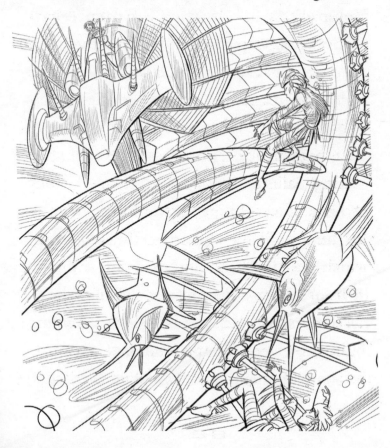

his hand on the creeper queen's head and spoke to her with his Aqua Powers. The queen gave a call, and Max watched as her sea ants swarmed over the massive Robobeast.

"Creepers!" sneered Iris. "Those miserable little insects are no danger to my magnificent Blistra!"

The Robobeast bucked and writhed, but the creepers gripped onto it with their claws and dipped their heads purposefully.

Resin!

"They're using resin! That stuff should put Blistra out of action!"

Lia nodded. "I think it's working!"

They could see the amber fluid flowing over the articulated joints, and setting there. Blistra's sinuous writhing was slowing down.

"No!" screamed Iris. The plasmagram burned with red light and leaned forward.

"She's commanding Blistra," said Max. "Its

mouth is opening!"

The Robobeast's snout flared open, revealing the fire building deep inside. "Duck!" Max cried to the Merryn. But instead of throwing flames forwards, the Robobeast folded back the ruff around its neck and bent its snake-like body so its head doubled back to face its tail. A jet of flames shot along the Robobeast's side. Immediately it swung its head the other way, and sent a plume of fire along its left side. Seawater boiled, and Max squinted against the heat, horrified as dozens of creepers burned up into blackened dust. The resin that had caked into Blistra's joints melted away, leaving its metal flanks clean and glowing with heat.

The Robobeast batted its wings, swatting some remaining creepers. Iris laughed. "You are no match for Blistra!"

Blistra turned back to the Merryn warriors

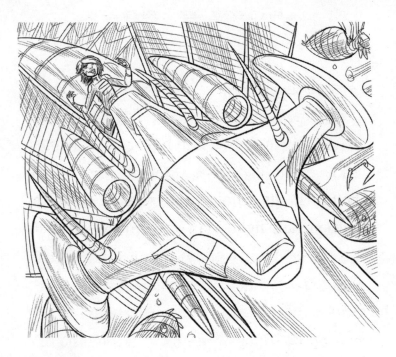

in front of it. Iris, too, stared at the massed army. She was smiling her cold smile. Max watched in horror as the Robobeast's eyes glittered dangerously. It fanned its ruff and spread its wings, and its snout flared wider. Fiery breath still burned deep in its throat.

It hasn't used up all its fuel!

"Look out!" Max cried. Blistra's head reared back, and at the same time its huge tail whipped out suddenly, smashing into the creeper queen. The insect was sent spinning away and King Salinas was flung from her back. Blistra roared and a torrent of flames shot from its throat, spraying the ocean before it. Its whole head seemed to burn with fire and light. Max was dimly aware that Rivet was dragging him out of the way. He flung his arm up to protect his eyes, but not before he'd seen Lia and Spike, zooming out of the path of the inferno.

When Max opened his eyes, the cooling water was full of burned and unconscious creeper bodies. Merryn were tending to their injured companions. King Salinas was unconscious, held by two Merryn, as Lia tried to wake him, while Spike swam next to her, trilling anxiously. Iris was already far in the distance, riding Blistra onwards. Max heard her cold metallic voice drifting back.

"Aquora will burn!"

CHAPTER EIGHT

THE DRAGON'S TREASURE

Max saw with relief that King Salinus was breathing, although his face was very pale. "Stay and look after your father," he said to Lia. "I'm going after Blistra." Lia nodded, barely looking up from her father's limp body.

Max grabbed Rivet's collar. "After them, Riv!"

Rivet set off, pulling Max through the water, his propellers whirring. They soon caught up with Blistra. The Robobeast was snaking through the ocean fast, but Rivet was faster.

As they approached the massive tail of the beast, Iris looked back and glared at Max. The plasmagram shimmered a deep, furious red. "I am getting bored with you!" she spat. The Robobeast lifted its wings at an angle and lowered its tail.

It's putting on the brakes, ready to turn and face me!

Max had no time to think. He let go of Rivet's collar, tensed his muscles and leapt. A millisecond later Blistra thrashed its great tail and twisted around. But Max had already landed on its back. He clung onto the metal scales, keeping his fingers away from the joints where the great armoured plates slid over each other like knives. The Robobeast writhed frantically, trying to shake Max off.

Its great wings snapped down and back up. They clanged against each other over the Robobeast's back, just missing Max.

"Enough!" shouted Iris. Blistra stopped thrashing and resumed its sinuous gliding swim towards Aquora. Max lifted his head. Iris was watching him from her seat on the Robobeast's neck. Suddenly, she flipped onto her feet, gracefully. She began walking along the long swaying spine of the Robobeast.

Perhaps I still have a chance to reason with her!

But Iris's right arm was beginning to change shape. Max stared in horror.

The liquid metal of the plasmagram arm was changing into something else. It grew longer and thinner. A sharp edge glinted. A sword!

Max took a shuddering breath. "Iris!" he shouted. "It's still not too late. The Aquorans

and Sumarans mean you no harm. Think! Use your logic!"

Iris paused, and Max rushed on. "You were damaged in the Primeval Sea. Your faulty programming is making you want to kill innocent people. I can help you. I can make you better..."

There was no dimming of the plasmagram's

fiery red sheen. Iris cocked her head and said, "I do not want your help. I am already 'better' than feeble biological organisms like you! I am true Artificial Intelligence! Not just programming, but a real person with emotions. And I have a burning desire to kill you!"

Max drew his hyperblade. It was made of vernium, the toughest known metal, but the thin blade looked fragile beside the plasmagram's fiery, red sword-arm.

Can I beat her? He steadied his feet on Blistra's back, adjusting his weight to the Robobeast's rippling movement.

Iris lunged with her sword, and Max swung his hyperblade against it. *Clang!* The blow sent a tremor through his arm, and his feet skidded over Blistra's metal plates. Iris followed up with a second lunge, and Max staggered as he blocked it. He recovered quickly, taking a deep breath and steadying both hands around the hilt of his hyperblade. He fought back, swinging his hyperblade with all his energy, but Iris parried every stroke, knocking Max's blade aside before it could touch her.

She's strong, and she won't get tired. But I will!

Max's gills were straining and his arm was heavy. It was getting harder to block Iris's relentless blows. Suddenly, Blistra's long body twitched, and Max lost his footing on the metal plates. He sprawled onto his back – *thump!* Iris stood over him, her sword-arm raised. Max tilted his hyperblade, but he had no strength left to protect himself.

I'm finished!

At that moment, Max saw a silver blur as Rivet barrelled into Iris, hitting her in the middle of her back. The plasmagram lurched

forwards. Max rolled aside, and Iris's sword just missed his neck. His own blade was still angled upwards, and Max felt a jolt as Iris landed on it. The blade sliced into her shoulder.

Iris pushed herself off the hyperblade and up onto her knees as Max wriggled away from her. He watched Iris's red glow fade to blue, then silver. The plasma sword blurred into the rough shape of an arm. But the arm was transparent.

She's fading!

The liquid metal was seeping out of Iris's shoulder wound and spreading like silver blood in the water.

Iris stared at Max. Her eyes still shone faintly with red light, but the rest of her was just a ghostly image. "My plasma body is dying," she hissed. "But Blistra is still under my control. My creation will not fail to destroy Aquora. He will blow it away with Infernium fire!"

Max shuddered at the faint, spiteful words. He raised his sword, and smashed it into the plasmagram. The liquid metal exploded into a shapeless cloud drifting away through the seawater. Her belt buckle sparked with

a few tiny red flashes and then dropped at
Max's feet. Blistra's sinuous glide through
the ocean did not falter. Max's tired legs
wobbled a little on the moving metal plates
as he bent and reached to pick up the silver
AI capsule, the source of Iris's life force. It
seemed inactive.

But this is her brain and heart, and it's still

giving orders to Blistra!

"Near Aquora, Max," Rivet warned, and Max remembered that the sea dragon was still heading towards the defenceless city.

It was easy to prise open the silver capsule, but the circuitry inside was more complex than anything Max had seen before.

I have to destroy it! He picked up his hyperblade and turned it to see it from the side. The vernium blade was so thin it almost disappeared. He took a deep breath and slid the graceful blade into the heart of the capsule.

Red fire sparked around the blade. At the same moment the Robobeast stalled, no longer urged on by the AI system. Max lurched forwards as the undulating movement beneath his feet came to an abrupt stop. The capsule flew out of his hand and skidded across Blistra's motionless back.

Rivet leapt into action.

"Fetched, Max!" he barked, wagging his tail happily.

Max burst out laughing. He felt his exhaustion drain away, replaced with a flood of relief.

It's over! I've stopped Blistra and defeated Iris!

"Thanks, Riv," he said, turning the capsule over in his hand. "Iris is in here, and I have a feeling this isn't quite the end of her!" He slipped the capsule into the chest pouch on his deepsuit. "And now we need to get the Infernium!"

The Robobeast's body was frozen like a vast metal sculpture, and its great wings hung half-open. Max swam over the sea dragon's back and landed at the front. There was a foot-long cylinder attached to its neck. *The battery pack!*

Max opened the pack. Tucked inside was a large ruby-red crystal. Max took the box out of Rivet's back-compartment. He wrapped his hands in a cloth to pick up the crystal of Infernium and then carefully placed the fourth element in its place with the others. He put back the box just as Lia rode up on Spike, calling his name.

Max was relieved to see the Sumaran army spread out behind Lia. Many of the

warriors were wounded and many were weaponless, their spears lost to Blistra, but they were riding proudly. Lia's father rode the creeper queen at the front of his army, with Lia beside him. The Merryn king's face was bruised, but no longer so pale. He lifted a hand to greet Max.

"What did I miss?" asked Lia with a broad smile. "I can see you've slain a dragon!"

Max grinned back. "And I found its treasure," he said. "It was guarding a big red jewel!"

"The Infernium?"

"Yep. The final ingredient." Max felt a rush of pride surge through his body. "You know what this means?"

Lia was laughing now. "We can restart Aquora's power core!"

Max nodded. Triumph welled up in his chest. "We've done it!"

CHAPTER NINE

POWER RESTORED

Max stood with his parents and Lia in the submerged chamber of Aquora's power core. He shivered inside his deepsuit. The chamber should have been blazing with energy from the central orb. But instead, without the pulsating plasma, this deep undersea place was as cold and dark as a tomb.

The beams from their torches gave glimpses of the chequerboard plates and

gaps that made up the chamber's cooling walls. The cylindrical column, strung with cables, still connected the orb to a shaft penetrating down into the sea bed. But without the four elements, the equipment could not tap heat from the centre of the planet to convert it into power. The orb was completely inert.

Max shivered again, a shudder of anxiety this time, rather than because of cold. He had a sudden, terrible thought; they had the four elements to restart the core...

But what if it doesn't work?

Callum laid a hand on Max's shoulder. Unlike Max and Niobe, Callum had never received the Merryn Touch and so couldn't breathe underwater. His voice crackled over the communicator in his amphibio mask. "It's time to meld the elements, Max. You do the honours."

Callum handed Max the box containing the elements, and Max twisted the dial on the top. The box didn't change, but Max knew that inside it the four elements, which had been stored in separate compartments until now, were reacting together. He passed the box to Rivet. "You know what to do, Riv."

The dogbot took the box carefully in his iron jaws. His snout and eye lamps shone like red torches as he swam up to the top of the power core and disappeared inside.

Moments later, Rivet reappeared without the box. Max let his breath out slowly as his dogbot swam back to him. "Well done, Riv," he whispered. "Will it work, Dad?" he added, turning to Callum.

"We must wait and see," said Callum. "This operation has never been performed before. But I hope so."

Niobe put an arm around Max's waist and gave him a quick hug. "Whatever happens," she said, "we know that we – you and Lia – have done everything possible."

"Do we need to wait here?" asked Lia.

"No," replied Callum. "We should be on the surface when the power starts up."

The group left the chamber and swam along the horizontal shaft to the open elevator. Max stepped onto the metal mesh platform and took hold of the handrail. "Magnetise paws, Riv," he commanded.

It would be crazy to get washed away now!

The elevator began to rise. Max looked up, but it was too dark to see the cables that were hauling it up towards the surface, powered by a standby battery system. Max kept staring upwards anyway, searching for a hint of light as the elevator lurched higher. It would be after sundown on the surface of Aquora by now.

But there won't be any lights until the power kicks in!

At last the elevator stopped. Max stumbled out after the others. As he'd expected, the building was dark, but he was glad to see the silver disk of Nemos's moon shining through the window.

Quickly, Max strode across the room and looked out. The city was plunged in darkness, but the shape of its skyline was clearly visible. It was silhouetted by the full moon and a stunning blaze of stars.

"Wow!" gasped Lia, at his side. "Your city looks much better with its lights switched off!" Suddenly serious, she added, "Don't worry. I'm sure the power will come back."

Max nodded grimly. *It has to.*

Suddenly, a crowd began pushing into the room, surrounding Callum and Niobe. Max was shocked to see the effects of the water rationing on the Aquorans. They were dirty and thirsty-looking. And they were clamouring for news that their ordeal was coming to an end.

"Did it work?"

"Why aren't the lights coming on yet?"

"Is the filtration system back?"

"Do we have water?"

Max saw Niobe lift her empty hands apologetically. One of the men wailed brokenly, "This is the end of us!" and others picked up the cry. The room filled with howling and sobbing.

Max was afraid the desperate people might attack Callum and Niobe. He began to push his way through the crowd to his parents.

But, before he could reach them, a flare of light burst up from the lift shaft. At the same time the building lights flickered, on, then off. Silence fell. Max held his breath with everyone else.

On again.

Max and Lia were almost trampled as people rushed to the door. Suddenly, Callum was at Max's side. "Come outside," he said. "You two should see this from the heart of the city."

Max glanced at Lia, and she grinned back at him. He called Rivet and they followed his parents into the open air.

Outside, people were streaming out of the buildings. One by one, the city lights blinked on. People shielded their faces from the glare, rubbing their dazzled eyes and laughing.

The streets, which had been so dark and quiet when Max returned from his battle with Blistra, were now humming with life. Street lamps and windows flickered and blazed, and there were muffled thumps as pipes and pumps started working again. Water began to sputter and glug from taps and fountains. Then it gushed.

Laughing, cheering people leapt into the ornamental fountains. They ducked under the water. They danced and splashed. They turned their mouths up to the water spouts, washing their faces and drinking the precious liquid, all at the same time.

"It's a good day for Breather technology," said Lia wryly, and Max's parents laughed.

"It certainly is," agreed Niobe. "The restored power core has saved the city and the lives of all the people!"

"Thanks to Lia and Max," added Callum, putting his arms around the three of them in a sudden fierce hug.

Just then somebody shouted, "There's the Chief Defence Engineer. It's Callum North!" and people began to crowd round, patting their backs and shaking their hands. Soon they were surrounded by excited people asking about the power and how the city had been saved.

"Time to slip away!" said Lia. She grabbed Max's hand and ran over to one of the fountains. Pulling Max down next to her, she sat on the edge and dabbled her webbed toes. Revelling children splashed them, and Max and Lia happily splashed back.

"I think that was our toughest Quest yet," said Max quietly. "There were times back then when I didn't think we'd make it. And now we're here, and the city's saved, and it feels so good!"

"It feels great, Max," agreed Lia. "I'd love to stay and celebrate, but I need to go back to Sumara to help resettle the creeper queen and her swarm. It's too far for them to travel home. I'll be back in no time. Who knows when we'll be needed for another Quest?"

Max nodded. "I have a feeling it won't be long. I hope you find a good place for the creepers."

"We will. The oceans are full of habitats. We'll find somewhere they fit perfectly!"

After Lia had said farewell to Callum and Niobe, Max and Rivet walked with her to the dock, waving her off, as she disappeared beneath the waves on Spike.

∘ ∘ ∘

Much later, in his bedroom in one of the tallest spires of Aquora, Max was listening to the Psychotic Sharks, turned down low so the music wouldn't disturb his parents. He was tinkering with something by the light of his desk lamp. After a while there

was a gentle knock at the door. Max dropped his hand under the desk, hiding what he was working on, as his mother peered into the room.

"I'm going to bed, Max," she said. "Get some rest too. It will be a busy day tomorrow. You need to submit a witness report to the council, telling them exactly what happened."

Max grimaced, and Niobe laughed. "Everyone will be keen to hear about your battle to save Aquora, and how you defeated that AI, Iris. They're already sending ships out to see if there's anything left of it. They'll find the wreckage of the *Liberty*, too, and the Robobeast, and salvage as much as they can." She paused. "I'm so proud of you, Max. It's good to have you home. Now get some sleep."

"Thanks, Mum. I'll go to bed soon, I promise."

Niobe closed the door behind her, and Max brought his hand back above the desk. He held Iris's control capsule up to the light. Max pulled on his magnifying goggles and chose a tool from his set of micro-screwdrivers. Then he continued working on the delicate circuitry.

Nearly finished...

Max had already identified and fixed the programming that had made Iris into a deranged psychopath. He had also managed to hook her up to the household network. Carefully he made the final connections. Then he closed the panel of the capsule, sat back and waited.

The capsule lit up with a rosy light, and a friendly voice said, "Hello, Max. What can I do for you?"

"Lights and music off, Iris!" commanded Max. The desk lamp turned off, and the music stopped.

It worked! Now I have my own obedient AI!

Max felt a moment of jubilation, and then suddenly very tired. Rivet was on the floor beside the bed. Max stepped over him and slid under the cover. "Goodnight, Riv. Goodnight, Iris."

"Night, Max," said Rivet.

"Goodnight, Max," said Iris.

Max closed his eyes. In the silence of the room, he could still hear the faint sound of people celebrating in the streets far below. He thought of Iris's Robobeasts. He had defeated them all: Veloth, Glendor, Mirrac and finally Blistra. He'd retrieved the elements and restored the core. The power was back. Aquora was saved.

Not bad! Of course, the seas of Nemos may not stay safe for long. Who knows how soon there might be another Quest...

Max smiled as he fell asleep.

Don't miss Max's next Sea Quest adventure,
when he faces

GORT
THE DEADLY
SNATCHER

SEA QUEST®

WIN AN EXCLUSIVE
GOODY BAG

In every Sea Quest book the Sea Quest logo is
hidden in one of the pictures. Find the logos in books
25-28, make a note of which pages they appear on and
go online to enter the competition at

www.seaquestbooks.co.uk

Each month we will put all of the correct entries into a draw
and select one winner to receive a special Sea Quest goody bag.

You can also send your entry on a postcard to:

Sea Quest Competition, Orchard Books,
Carmelite House, 50 Victoria Embankment,
London, EC4Y 0DZ

Don't forget to include your name and address!

GOOD LUCK

Closing Date: May 31st 2016